It's Kwanzaa Time!

A Lift-the-Flap Story

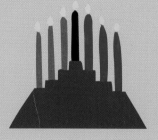

By Synthia Saint James

LITTLE SIMON
An imprint of Simon & Schuster Children's Publishing Division
New York   London   Toronto   Sydney   Singapore
1230 Avenue of the Americas, New York, New York 10020
Copyright © 2001 by Synthia Saint James
LITTLE SIMON and colophon are registered trademarks of Simon & Schuster.
Manufactured in China   ISBN 0-689-84163-9   First Edition
2 4 6 8 10 9 7 5 3 1

On December 26, Kwanzaa begins. We celebrate the seven days and the seven principles of Kwanzaa.

Umoja (oo•MOH•jah) is today's principle. It means "unity."

We celebrate togetherness
with friends . . .

On the second day of Kwanzaa we celebrate the principle of *Kujichagulia* (koo•jee•chah•goo•LEE•ah), which means "self-determination."

On the third day of Kwanzaa
we celebrate the principle of
Ujima (oo•JEE•mah), which means
"working together."

Together we know that . . .

On the fourth day of Kwanzaa we celebrate
the principle of *Ujamaa* (oo•jah•MAH•ah),
which means "helping each other."

We help to keep our neighborhoods good, safe, . . .

On the fifth day of Kwanzaa we celebrate
the principle of *Nia* (NEE•ah), which means
"purpose."

On the sixth day of Kwanzaa we celebrate
the principle of *Kuumba* (koo•OOM•bah),
which means "creativity."

We make music, sing, dance, color, . . .

On the seventh day of Kwanzaa we celebrate
the principle of *Imani* (ee•MAH•nee), which
means "faith."

We have faith in ourselves, in our families . . .

It's Kwanzaa time! Happy, Happy Kwanzaa!